For Jack
M·E·

For Bonnie
G·R·

Reprinted 1996

First published in 1996 by Magi Publications
22 Manchester Street, London W1M 5PG

This edition published 1996

Text © 1996 Mark Ezra
Illustrations © 1996 Gavin Rowe

Mark Ezra and Gavin Rowe have asserted their rights
to be identified as the author and illustrator of this work under
the Copyright, Designs and Patents Act, 1988.

Printed and bound in Belgium by Proost N.V., Turnhout

ISBN 1 85430 398 8

MARK EZRA

The Hungry Otter

pictures by GAVIN ROWE

Little Otter was feeling hungry.
"I'll go out to catch some fish," he said,
and before any of his brothers or sisters noticed
what he was doing, he launched himself out of his
bankside home and down into the water . . .

. . . but the water was not there!
Instead there was a glassy surface of solid ice.
Little Otter went slithering and skidding over it,
his paws scrabbling helplessly.

At last Little Otter was able to get to his feet.
He looked around him and saw nothing but
white snow where the fields and green
meadows had once been. It all looked so
strange and unfamiliar.

Little Otter ran and jumped around in the snow for a while, and then he bounded off along the riverbank to find the mud slide where his family played each evening before sunset. He passed high hedges, frosted white, and crossed a lane with deep frozen ruts.

Little Otter soon found the mud slide,
but it was set iron hard.
A large crow was already there,
his feathers puffed out against the cold.

The crow flopped over on his back,
stuck his spindly legs in the air
and scooted down the slide and on to
the ice with a joyful croak.

"That's *my* slide," Little Otter was about to cry
indignantly, but then something caught his eye.
He saw a fox, silently creeping towards the crow.
The fox kept his body low and out of sight.
        The crow was so busy enjoying himself that
            he didn't see the danger.
                Closer and closer the fox crawled,
                        until suddenly. . .

. . . the fox pounced.
At the same time, Little Otter
gave a cry of warning.

The crow flapped his wings and took off into
the branches of a tree, just as the fox snapped
at his tail feathers.

Then the fox slipped and skidded down the
slide and across the ice.

Defeated, he picked himself up and loped off
angrily across the fields.

"Thank you," said the crow. "You saved my life. But what are you doing here?"

"I came to find my mud slide," said Little Otter. "And now I'm very hungry, because I can't catch any fish. The river is all frozen over."

"That's easy to put right," said the crow.

"Just leave it to me."

The crow picked
up a large stone
in his beak,

flew high over the water, and dropped it.
With a loud CRACK it fell through the ice.

"There you are," said the crow. "Now you
have a hole and can fish. Come to think of it,
I'm pretty hungry, too, so while you're at it,
catch one for me!"

Little Otter dived
into the water and
caught a fish for
the crow. . .

. . . but when he
went back to get
one for himself,
he found the
fish were alert.
They were not so
easy to catch.

Little Otter chased the fish downstream,
till at last he caught another one.
But when he tried to swim to the surface,
he could not find the hole!
Little Otter clawed at the ice, trying to
break through. He saw the blue sky above him,
but the thick ice lay between him and the fresh air.
Just as he thought he would drown in the freezing
water, he saw a black shape, high above him.

CRACK!
A heavy stone smashed through the ice,
making another hole.

Holding his fish, Little Otter scrambled out
of the river and lay on the bank, gasping for air.
The crow hopped over to him.
"One good turn deserves another," he said.
"You saved my life, and I saved yours!"

The crow flew back up to his perch to
finish off his fish, and Little Otter shook
his spiky fur dry.
Then, dragging his own fish behind him,
he made his way back home.

"A fish!" cried Little Otter's brothers and sisters. "How did you catch a fish when the river is frozen over?"
And, as the hungry family sat down to eat it, Little Otter told them his story . . .